Who wants to be a *poodle*

I don't

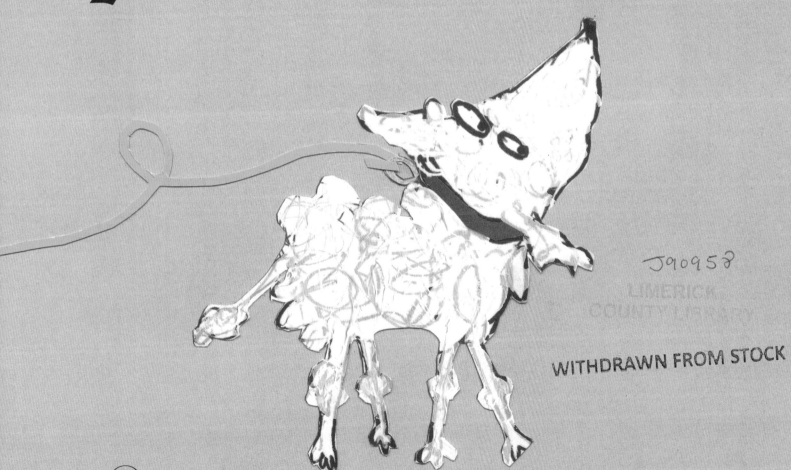

PUFFIN

lauren child

A Cautionary Tale
for Verity

who would love nothing better
than to dress her cat in a little bonnet

PUFFIN BOOKS   Published by the Penguin Group: London, New York, Australia, Canada, India, Ireland, New Zealand and South Africa   Penguin Books Ltd, Registered Offices: 80 Strand, London WC2R 0RL, England   puffinbooks.com   First published 2009   This edition published 2011   Text and illustrations copyright © Lauren Child, 2009   All rights reserved   The moral right of the author/illustrator has been asserted   Made and printed in Malaysia   ISBN: 978-0-141-50246-5   001 – 10 9 8 7 6 5 4 3 2 1

IN
a sumptuous apartment in a
fashionable city lived the elegantly rich and
divinely glamorous Mademoiselle Verity Brulée.

Verity Brulée did little with her time but shop for shoes
and visit the beauty parlour to have her wrinkles
smoothed and her eyelashes
lengthened.

She was the kind of person who liked   everything to be 'just so'.

ALONG with Verity Brulée, with her very own personal bedroom,
lived **Trixie Twinkle Toes Trot-a-lot Delight**
   or **Trixie Toes** for short
   or **Trixie Twinkle Belle**
   or **Trixie Belle Baby**,
depending on Verity's mood.

The little poodle lived in the
lap of luxury with every creature
comfort just a manicured paw away.

There was a maid to plump her cushions

and
a cook
to prepare
her n i b b l e s

and a butler to carry her over the puddles.

And she was much adored
by Mademoiselle Brulée.

BUT Trixie Twinkle Toes was not happy.
For a start, she didn't like her name,
it was far too poodley.

She didn't like
the
puffing

or the
poofing

or the
preening.

She didn't like the posing or the prancing.

She didn't like
the perfuming
the powdering
or the pompoms.

And she didn't like the way her owner
Verity Brulée would keep dressing
her up in little pink ponchos.

THE thing was, Trixie Twinkle Toes just wasn't a poodle sort of person.
'No, I am just not cut out for a life of poodlery,
I want to step in puddles.'

But of course she
kept these thoughts to herself.

Mademoiselle Verity Brulée never went out if the weather
was wet or indeed cloudy, stormy, snowy or in fact
anything but fine. Her shoes were very expensive
and she could not risk them getting spoilt.

This meant
the two of them
were usually stuck
inside their
apartment —

Verity Brulée
idly flicking
through shoe
catalogues,

while
Trixie Twinkle Toes
would chew on her pink
velvet ribbon.

And it was an uneventful life for both of them.

ON fine days the two of them would go out prancing in the park, though Verity never permitted the little poodle to stray from the path for fear of muddy paws. Trixie Twinkle Toes

'That's what a REAL dog should do,' she would think, sighing a deep sigh.

would peer over at the other dogs scampering about with sticks, paddling in puddles and chasing nothing in particular.

Mademoiselle Brulée often mistook these sighs for little coughs and would wrap another little scarf around poor Trixie Twinkle Toes' neck.

ONE night Trixie Twinkle Toes was lying in her room,
listening to the real dogs howling at the moon.
As far as she could tell
they were all called
names like

Growler
and
Gripper
and
Chomper
and
Squasher.

'That's what a dog's name should be,' thought Trixie Twinkle Toes, looking into her full-length mirror, but what she saw just didn't look like someone who would ever be called Squasher. Pompommed toy poodles just aren't.

'I hate being a poooodle,'

she howled in a most
un-poodle-like fashion.

WHICH woke Mademoiselle Brulée from her anxious dreams.

She popped on her kitten-heeled mules and clip-clacked her way down the corridor.

VERITY Brulée took a good look at
Trixie Twinkle Toes Trot-a-lot Delight and said,
'Heavens, what is the matter with you,
my forlorn furry friend?'

And she rang for the maid,

who summoned the vet, who after concocting

many tests and treatments could find nothing wrong with the little dog.

Other than a slightly sore throat.

fleas flee

To cheer her up, the following day Verity Brulée took
Trixie Twinkle Toes to the poodle parlour, *Hound Heaven*.

Whilst under the dryer, idly flicking through
the latest issue of *Posh Pooch Monthly*,

she noticed an article titled
How to Change your Dog Image.

It showed a photograph of an unruly,
scruffy-looking dog and next to it a
picture of the same dog all neat and tidy
and the words *three months later.*

'Of course,' she thought, 'if a dog can be
cleaned and preened then it can also
be scruffed and roughed.'

'I will change my image,' she said,
as she sipped her cappoochcino.

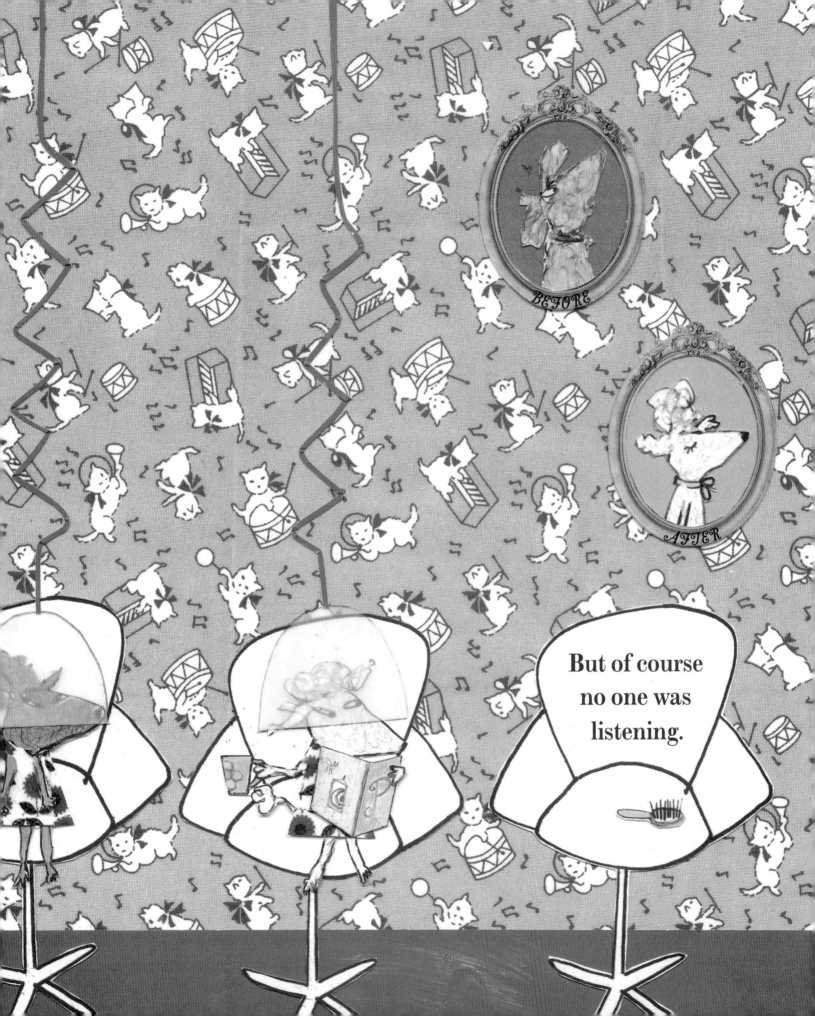

BEFORE

AFTER

But of course
no one was
listening.

THE very next day

Trixie Twinkle Toes

chased a cat,

caught

some fleas

and

chewed Mr Chomley's newspaper.

Verity Brulée, utterly alarmed, telephoned her pet psychic to see if she could find out just what strange force was troubling her little dog.

MR Agunadi looked
into Mademoiselle
Verity
Brulée's
teacup
but could see
nothing
but

two
lonely
tea leaves.

Then he looked at

VERITY Brulée had
Trixie Twinkle Toes
kept indoors,
de-flea-ed

and given another
helping of the finest
dishy dog food.

Trixie Twinkle Toes felt relieved.
She found cats boring, fleas itchy and newspapers rather bland.

ONE rainy day later,
Trixie Twinkle Toes was
idly watching TV when up popped
a commercial for

THE GREATEST
DOG ACT
ON EARTH.

The voice said,

'BE ASTOUNDED
BE AMAZED
BE BAMBOOZLED
BY THE PERFORMING
POODLE SISTERS!'
And then she saw
the words

DAZZLINGLY
DANGEROUS
DARING DOGS!

Trixie Twinkle Toes had never even heard of
a poodle being DANGEROUS or DARING
but she liked the idea of it.

'I will become DANGEROUS and DARING,' she said, hopping off her pile of feather cushions.

But who would believe such a thing, even if they had been listening.

On Tuesday the doorman caught Trixie Twinkle Toes sliding down the banisters.

Mr Eccles thought he saw her swinging

on the chandelier

and Mrs Grover, the dog walker, swore she spotted Trixie Twinkle Toes diving into the ornamental fountain.

VERITY Brulée,
shocked by this
astonishing
behaviour,
rang
down
to
the
doorman
who
ordered
a car to drive
Trixie Twinkle Toes
Trot-a-lot Delight
to the pooch
psychiatrist

on
the
double!

Qu

iCk! Step on it!

THE psychiatrist got
Trixie Twinkle Toes
to do some very
tricky tests.

He even tried
hypnosis but he just
could not discover
what was wrong.

At last, exasperated, he sighed,
'What is the trouble,
my small
canine
client?'

'I want to
stick my head out of
car windows and feel
the wind in my ears.

I want to bark at dogs in the street.

I want to catch sticks
and roll in the mud.

I want to be DANGEROUS and DARING

but most of all

I want

to step

in puddles.'

But of course the psychiatrist could not understand her.

By the time they stepped out of the psychiatrist's office the rain was pouring down and beautiful pools of water were forming everywhere.

Trixie

looked

longingly

at the

deep

grey

puddles

but

said

nothing.

Until suddenly Trixie Twinkle Toes heard a terrible sound.

It was the howl of a tiny drowning hound.

In one DAZZLING moment she slid down the railings, took a DARING leap into the air, and DANGEROUSLY dived into the deepest puddle. Verity Brulée, fearing her little dog was in great danger, waded in after her, instantly ruining her shoes.

BUT to Verity's astonishment
there was Trixie Twinkle Toes not drowning
but holding up the bedraggled chihuahua.

'What a DOG!'
exclaimed the owner.
'You have saved
little Gripper
from certain
death.'

Verity Brulée looked at Trixie Twinkle Toes and saw not a little pompommed toy poodle but instead a

DAZZLINGLY
DANGEROUS
DARING
dog.

Trixie Twinkle Toes barked, and suddenly Verity Brulée understood every word.

FROM that day on
Mademoiselle Verity Brulée
and Trixie Twinkle Toes eagerly
read the weather pages — and if it
was raining … they went out …
with all the other dogs.

And Verity
never made Trixie
Twinkle Toes wear
a hat, a scarf or even
a poncho ever again.

Though however much Trixie Twinkle Toes tried, she just could not get Verity to understand one important thing . . .

'Trixie Twinkle Toes Trot-a-lot Delight!'

...DAZZLINGLY
DANGEROUS
DARING dogs
do not like to be called silly names.